# FoxFire

## Sisters of the Fae, Volume 1

Clair Gardenwell

Published by Clair Gardenwell, 2020.

FOXFIRE

**First edition. December 9, 2020.**



ISBN: 978-1393260714

Written by Clair Gardenwell.

# Table of Contents

# 1



"**I**f we lower the taxes on the farmer's water by 10%, the increase of the field's yield will more than double their current state." I explained to the snarling high lords of my own Wind court. My shoulders were slim but I shifted them back as straight as a soldiers and narrowed my already narrow set eyes. There was several people that said I was an intimidating person despite my slender build, but unfortunately for me, none of those people were currently present.

The currently assembled aristocrats viewed my every movement and word with a venomous scorn not only dripping from their eyes but from their lips as well, the proud broad feathered wings subtly flexing behind their backs in a show of stoic solidarity was the hallmark of our proud court. The Wind Court, fleetest of all Fae and certainly the most intelligent of all the Fae courts. "Thank you for your ideas, princess. It certainly gives us something to think about. Now, why don't you run along and help your sister with the party? It's only in two days that you'll both turn nineteen. It's truly a momentous occasion and should be celebrated properly." The tallest of them all spoke, his drooping grey streaked mustache muffling his words.

I gave my most disgusted glance to all of them before swiveling on my heel, the loosened strands of my straight brunette hair flying free from the knot braided securely at the nape of my neck, only coming to dangle between the protruding edges of my razor sharp shoulder blades that bore no sign of the Wind Court's proudest symbol. The feathered wings that propelled them through the sky. My sister and I's birth was supposed to be a symbol of hope for the Wind Court, but instead our names were cursed as the ill-fated match between the highest of the Wind Fae lords and his most favored human servant. The results were ourselves, the children of such a union, having the thin build and pale coloring of the Wind Fae, but with no magical abilities and certainly no wings to support us. An affront to the regal court whose magical abilities were as highly prized as the wings.

Publicly, both I and my sister along with our mortal mother were supported by the full reach of the Court, but privately we were treated as nothing more than dolls barely fit to command the throne. A fact that I am so determined to change after my nineteenth birthday and I inherit the crown of High Lady to share with my sister.

If only I can make sure that my sister's feeble mind doesn't stray from the path.

I charged through the palace halls on my way to the garden, quickly brushing past each and every servant that crossed my path along the way till a single solid hand landed on my shoulder stopped me cold.

"Where are you going in such a hurry, Princess?" A thick but soft, Souji's voice was one like the gentle puff of a summer's breeze. Thick and warm just like himself with a lazy rhythm that belayed his truth nature. Dressed in the navy and brown uniform of a captain in the royal army leagues, Souji had been both personal guard and our attendant for as long as I could remember, even going so far as to call him a friend despite being our elder by a year. Born a Fire Fae with the slanted features and broad build, his Fae features of twitching pointed ears stationed atop his short shorn blonde hair streaked with golden red, nine twisting tails constantly twitching and shifting from the base of his spine out to the length of his shoulders in a shape similar to a fox's own tail, and his purely golden eyes that shone like the most polished metal darkened only by the slitted expanse of his ebony pupil. Yes, Souji was a favorite by all of the ladies for his classically handsome looks, but none more so than my sister.

"I'm going to speak with my idiot sister." I pulled away from his hand with a rough shake of my shoulders.

"Aw, Lissa. Don't be like that. She's just excited about the party." He crossed his arms over his broad chest, a boyish smile twisting his features into a charming grin while his eyes glowed with a glimmer of amusement twinkling like a star. A lesser woman might have fell victim to his charms, but not me.

"Sister, look here! Isn't it beautiful?" A call from the distance made me turn away from Souji and towards the light green dress bedecked figure in the distance. The younger princess of the court spread her arms wide to gesture over the lavishly decorated space of what formed the guardian of the royal palace. As different from my own self as day was to night. Belima's thin build was all smiles with bubbling blue eyes and long hair the color of the golden sunlight paired well with a flawless complexion to easily make her a more cheerful reflection of our mortal mother whereas I resembled the stern features of our Fae father.

"Oh, how I wish that your father was here to see this. He would be so proud of you." The high lady, our mother, stepped out from the shadows of the hall and wiped away a tear with the tip of her sleeve. Dressed in a long gown of fluttery sky blue fabric and golden emblements, my mother was truly beautiful with her long blonde hair dangling free about her shoulders and a beaming smile on her face. She looked much too happy for such an occasion.

"Father would be reigning terror down on the heads of the statesmen for daring to oppose him." I crossed my arms over my chest and viewed the scene with a skeptical eye. It looked like someone had tossed paper streamers throughout the green expansion of the garden. Trees, shrubs, and flowers, not a single surface had been spared from the colorful assault till it looked like a unicorn had thrown up everywhere.

"Sco-Sco! Get down from there!" Belima scolded suddenly. Intertwined deep in the tangled strings of petite paper lanterns, a small dragon snapped and growled at his bonds, his tiny limbs flailing and jerking more of the lanterns loose with every twirl of his sinuous cobra like body. Scolies was my sister's pet and beloved companion, one of the few tame dragons in existence. Belima rushed to his side, swiftly untangling the small dragon while my mother and Souji looked on with a bubble of light laughter.

"Fools, they view us all as fools and they are right." I couldn't resist muttering. No matter what we do, the court was never going to view us as nothing more than fools.

"Relax, Lissa. It's just Scolies's usual antics. No harm done." Souji tried to lighten my somber mood with a quick smile. "In two days, you're going to be high lady and this will all be forgotten." Belima continued to coax the little dragon down from his nest of string and festive paper lanterns made special for the occasion.

"Don't call me Lissa!" I snapped.

"Whatever, your highness." He executed a light bow, one that had a stray strand of his curly hair falling over his eyes and I couldn't bring myself to stay mad for long. My friendship with the fire court origin man was too long standing for a mere brief disagreement to retain too much of a prickle.

"I hope you're right." Even as the words left my lips, I wished down to my very bones that it was true, but I had a sneaking suspicion that it wasn't.

# 2



It was the darkest hour of the night when something shook away the threads of sleep and pulled me into wakefulness. "Wake up!" My eyes flew open, immediately seeing the fully widened expanse of my mother's fear widened ones leaning over my head. "Avalissa, we must go and quickly!" Before I could even take a breath, she pulled me away from the warmth of my bed and rushed me straight into the waiting hands of Souji.

The princesses' guard was blood spattered and snarling, his trusted sword in hand and the full flames of his fire magic blazing bright and dripping in streams of liquid orange fire from his arms. Coiling up and around his tails, the orange fire brightened even more into a hue nearly eye burning in its brightness, but it wasn't matched at all by the glow of power in his eyes. Burning like lit coals themselves, I couldn't help but wonder what type of foe had awakened such power in him as he normally preferred to be so calm and easygoing rather than showing the flaming core of his power.

Huddled small in the shadows of her own bed, Belima desperately clutched at the shivering Scolies wrapped around her arm, her white nightgown adding a layer of ghostly essence to her already pale tone until she looked like a phantom herself. My mother paid no heed though as she pushed us all up and away with quick, hurried motions. Like a dark wrath of flame himself, Souji slunk in the lead, more than a few unwary screams being cut short with the neat hiss of his blade cleaving through flesh and bone. Thick talons of pure horror ripped sharp and quick through my chest as I watched the edge of a black clad man's body fall into our line of sight. "Bandits are attacking the castle! We need to sound the alarm!" I shouted, reaching for the blade of enchanted Fae steel that I normally kept by my waist, only to remember that I was in my nightgown. I started to shout again, but my mother's hand quickly clapped tight over my mouth in the same instant that she pressed a blade into my hands.

"Quiet! They are assassins sent to kills us all." She hissed directly into my ear. With a strong push, Belima's shoulder crashed into mine as we both staggered forward a step. Confused, I tossed a glance over my shoulder to see her standing there with the glaze of unshed tears glistening bright in her eyes. "Now, the two of you listen and listen well. Go to the Dusk Court and speak to the High Lord there. Tell him who you are and what has happened. He will help you. Now remember, you are each as strong as the strongest of the Fae. Just remember your own strengths and keep hope. Be brave and be strong against the tides of fate, but most importantly, never forget who you are and what you can do." Once finished, the High Lady of the Wind Court turned towards a newly returned Souji, placing her hands on his broad shoulders and pulling him down for a hug that smeared scarlet blood across the hem of her gown. "Take care of my girls and yourself." I barely heard her whisper.

Souji murmured something that sounded like thank you, but before I could even blink again, he had gathered us each in each arm and led us away into the dark of the night.

"Mother! What are you doing?" I screamed out, the sudden flash of a silver blade nearly clipped my ear from my head as someone appeared from the dark but immediately found their end at the end of short silver sword in my mother's hand.

"Defending my court, darling." The High Lady of the Wind Court called out to me as more of the dark clad people came to the fore and she vanishing into the fray. The sharp clear ring of Fae steel clanged against Fae steel, the drumbeat of powerful wings clapping through the air like thunder as more descended from the moonlit skies above. It was not simply assassins or any ordinary bandits that had descended on the court, but the very Wind Court itself was fighting against each other.

As she watched the fire Fae boy she had raised as her own lead her daughters away, the High Lady turned and faced the rising threat with her bloodstained weapon bared and ready to plunge into the next fleshy target. "You are a brave one. As foolish as your husband, but brave. It's too bad that bravery will be waster." The trusted adviser that had served so faithfully at her husband and her daughters' side, Marolik Drakenburg, purred as he drifted down on silent wings with a long sword of his own extended to chop her head from her shoulders. The High Lady crossed her sword over her chest, blocking the blow that might have killed another weaker person but not her. She fought the advisor with everything she had, her only thought being to buy enough time for the Wind Courts twin hopes to flee before the Fae steel sliced her from shoulders to stomach. Her final thought being the faces of her daughters and the hopes that perhaps one day, they would indeed be the vision of hope that she had always knew they would be.

# 3



~Belima~

"**P**lease, my ladies! You must hurry!" Souji urged my failing legs on, but I was so tired. This had to be a nightmare. My home, my mother, it couldn't all be gone in just a puff of smoke.

"Souji! We shouldn't be running but fighting!" Avalissa paused just ahead of me, stamping her slipper clad feet against the dirt in protest while the drumbeat of wings continued to sound from somewhere behind us. Her fists, pale and thin with the bones outlined beneath her skin like miniature swords underneath her skin, were clenched tied at her sides like she was intending to fight them herself with her bare fists and the blade in her hand.

With Souji's presence urging us on, we were quickly pushed into a small thicket of trees so dense that I couldn't see anything but the needle sharp leaves around me. At least the wingbeats had stopped for now, fading into the distance until the distinctive thrumming was barely nothing more than a distant boom.

Finally we stopped as the trees opened up into a small clearing, Souji clearing a small space aside that he lit a small fire with a single spark. I slumped against the trunk of a tree, the rough bark clawing at my back but I didn't really care. The only home I had ever know had just went up in flames. I could still the dark clothed ones slinking through every corner of the palace that I had explored myself in some silent mockery of everything that I had known as normal was now gone. Scolies shivered in my arms, his shimmering scales gone dark and cold with his fright. The color shifting ability of small dragons like Scolies were meant to protect them from predators, but it was also a useful indicator of how he felt as well.

Glancing across the fire, Avalissa sat against her own tree in solemn silence. Her eyes were cold and hard, gazing into the dancing flames of the fire like she wanted to strangle the life from it herself. I could see the inner workings of her mind churning and I could practically predict what she was thinking of. The betrayal by one that we had never expected to come. It wasn't long before I could feel my eyelids drooping with the weight of sleep, and I hugged Scolies's body closer to my chest before falling prey to its claws.

As dusk turned to dawn, so did a sense of tentative peace achieve with the chirping return of the wildlife and the swift breeze singing through the weighted limbs of the trees.

Sadly it wasn't the sweet song of the birds that was trying to wake me up, but a foot shoving hard against my shoulders. "Get up." Avalissa growled, jabbing the bony heel of her foot right into the joint of my shoulder before she stalked off with the filthy edge of her nightgown swirling around her legs. I blinked wearily, my eyes stinging and probably red rimmed from my earlier tears, and the soft but still severe bite of the wind causing a fresh bout of water to fall free from my eyes.

"We've got to find shelter and raise a force to take back the court." Avalissa's voice drew my attention towards the fire where she stood with her hands planted firmly on her hips, staring Souji down with a power that should have crushed the will of a weaker man.

Instead of being frightened, Souji was lazily stirring the dying embers of the fire with a blackened stick, pausing only to casually glance up at my sister in question. "Lissa, you're already planning an attack on the adviser? With what army?"

"Once we reach city of Lotare, I will make an announcement of what's happened and ask that all those citizens join me and spread the word about the attack. We will rise up with an army of our own and take back the court!" Avalissa declared triumphantly, her fists shaking high in the air with the force of her fury.

She was really considering doing that? "You'll be killed before you even speak your first word." I muttered softly, my fingers idly tracing over the patter of a sleeping Scolies smooth scales. He hadn't moved throughout the whole night. "The people hate us, and they would never follow us. You know that."

This time she rounded on me, the full weight of her fury dripping from her venomous tongue as she let loose a new scathing reply. "Do you have a better idea bedsides sitting around and waiting for them to kill us?"

"We could do as mother suggested and go to the dusk court."

Avalissa scoffed. "Those backwater night rats? We would be better off trying to contact one of our allies, the Dawn Court or the Water court."

"Most likely they are already in league with the adviser himself." Souji commented idly, the constant scratching of the stick against the softly glowing coals quickly growing irritating even to my ears.

"There is always the fire court?" Avalissa ticked off on her fingers.

"Not if you value your life. They would betray their own life for the money." The sudden brusqueness in Souji's easy voice was so sharp that even Scolies roused from his slumber. He raised his head up from where it had propped on my thigh, glancing over at the Souji's twitching ears and twisting tails with a curious cheep of wonder.

"Fine then," My sister spat, eyeing Souji with a cautious eye like one would do a snake about to strike. "What about the Earth Court?"

Souji shook his head. "Too far away. I made a promise to the queen to keep you both safe and the Dusk Court will supply that. It will be dangerous as we will have to cross both Wind and Water territory, so tell me now if you will."

His words sunk in slowly, but we both nodded in sync. After all, we had no other choice.

# 4

~Belima~

It shouldn't have been much of a surprise that we weren't quite used to the ways of the forest, but it was still so frustrating I accidentally set fire to the immediate surroundings of Souji's campfire when he instructed me to simply push dirt over the smoldering embers to make sure it was out, even singing the tips of Avalissa's hair with the flames. That only increased Avalissa's ire as she constantly kept reprimanding me for my clumsiness, but it only made my hands shake even more.

"Souji! Where is the blade I brought with me?" Avalissa demanded sharply.

"Right here," With a quick flick of one pointed tail tip, Souji pointed to where a single blade was sheathed safely along the belt around his waist.

Her face turned a shade of scarlet so deep that her face flushed straight from her cheekbones to the base of her neck. "Give it to me!" She held out her hand in waiting along with her demand.

"Princess, as much as I do appreciate your eagerness, you're not getting a blade that you can't handle." He pulled out a small dagger clipped to the back of his belt. "Try this, it's much more suited for you."

Her lip curled with a degree of skepticism usually reserved for only the most foul of concoctions that our chef came up with... or used to come up with. "A dagger? Really? What do you expect me to do? Tickle a foe with it?"

Souji's expression flattened into a serious scowl. "No. I would expect you to defeat them with it."

My feet tangled together as I started to rise from my seat on a fallen log, my stomach hitting the ground with a fleshy thump against the ground that drove the breath from my lungs in a quick rush. Out of the corner of my eye I noticed that Avalissa had swung her venomous gaze towards me. "Seriously, can she not even walk?" Avalissa's scathing criticism drew tears my eyes with a powerful sting until I felt warm hands raise up my shoulders and lift me to my feet like I was nothing.

"It's okay, Princess. Don't cry. Did you hurt yourself?"

"No. I'm fine." I crushed my hands against my tear stained cheeks.

"Easy Princess." He pulled out a handkerchief from a pocket hidden somewhere in his uniform and gently wiped against my cheek. The pale fabric came away stained with a dark smear of "Much better." He smiled softly.

"Would you stop babying her! How do you expect her to survive if you keep hovering over her like some kind of nursemaid?" Souji stood, meeting Avalissa eye to eye and not wavering in the least bit from her imposing stance.

"That is something I wanted to tell you both. As for my own appearance, I can disguise myself well enough, but the two of you are entirely too recognizable. That's why I picked these up." He pulled two chunks of clear quartz looped by a tough leather string out, the opaque stones looking almost delicate in his large hands. "With your permission princesses, I can cast an illusion spell to alter your features so that you will be unrecognizable."

"Go ahead." Avalissa snapped with a wave of her hand. Balanced in the center of his palm, the quartz crystals burned hot with an inner orange light as he used his unique magic to cast and store an image into the crystal. One finished, the stone flickered and shimmered with the dancing light of an inner fire. As soon as I felt the cord and crystal slip around my neck, the image fell over my face like a veil as the glamor took hold. It was true what they said, Fire Fae were unparalleled in creating glamours.

"Now we can leave." He murmured solemnly before adjusting his own disguise. We were clad only as a batch of dirty faced travelers, but I hope that we could avoid notice for too long.

# 5



It was more difficult than it looked to remain in hiding once we reached Cotare, but Souji certainly underestimated the population that the trading post would have in attendance. Even as distraught as my sister was, she still couldn't resist the lure of an Earth Court trader come to sell his wares. I waited in the distance, impatiently tapping my fingers against my hip while she fingered gently over the array of glittering necklaces and bracelets. She had at least two pairs of each kind back at home, but she must have thought about that because she suddenly burst out into tears. Souji quickly swept her away, his cloak flaring around her like a protective shield as he tucked her away against his chest, offering the staring merchant an uneasy smile before swearing sharply under his breath as I turned and started to stalk away.

I wove through the meandering crowd, one hand resting on the dagger sheathed at her waist and keeping a steady eye on the patrolling soldiers that wove through the crowd. I couldn't help but stifled a groan of disgust every time I saw my family's coat of arms emblazed on the chest of the same ones who had sworn loyalty to my family, but laughed and jeered at their demise.

I had a particular one in my sights, his loudly mocking mouth never stopped flapping and his raucous laughs brayed like a donkey's call. He never shut up, not even to take a breath, and I wrapped my hands around the hilt of my blade and crept forward on silent feet. My combat training was one thing that my father had made sure we both were trained in before he died, but somehow I missed when a hand landed on my shoulder. As quick as a viper's strike, I slashed out with my dagger only to be disarmed with a quick flick of the wrist.

"Stop it and come on. It's not worth it!" Souji growled.

I grumbled a curse under my breath, sheathing the knife as Souji led us onward to a small inn. With a quick smile and a flash of coins, a room was captured for the night and for the next few days to come. Small and shabby, the two twin beds were the highlight of the room and not much else. It was a far cry from our homes at the castle, but Belima barely gave the room a half glance before she settled on the bed closet to the wall, curling into a ball with her knees tucked up tight to her chest. I couldn't calm the restless feeling surging through my legs, itching to walk and wander, I started pacing the length of the room back and forth while Souji settled what few belongings we had in place.

"I'm going into town for supplies. Will you two be alright?" His words were aimed more towards more me, but his worried gaze never left my sister's huddled form. Faintly I noticed Scolies had curled himself in the space between her shoulder and her neck, the little dragon making worried little clucking noises over the state of his mistress.

"Go on! We'll be fine." I tossed a disgusted glance down at the current mud, filth, and grime crusted state of my dress. "And find me a new dress as well."

"Yes, Lissa." The ghost of a smile played across his features as he departed along with a hissed screech of his name from my lips as he called me that name once again. I hated that name, but he refused to forget what had once been a childhood nickname and was certainly not fit for a princess to bear.

Soon after his departure, the room grew quiet except for the hushed scuffle of my footsteps. I heard the shuttered gasps and the tears of Belima's shoulder shaking sobs. Scolies chirps grew louder in volume with the force of his worry, his tiny forked tongue reaching out to lick his mistress tears away while he snuggled beneath her chin.

"Stop it! Just stop it!" I snarled, reaching out to slap my sister's hands away from my face. How dare she sit around and cry when we had so much work to be done. "You've done nothing but squall like a baby since we left!"

Belima babbled nonsense, her tongue twisted with sobs to even try and even defend herself. Scolies growled a warning, thin needle like spikes rising in a ruff around his oblong head. Even as a pet, a dragon's loyalty was something to be feared.

"That's enough, Avalissa. Leave your sister be." Sometime during our encounter, I had failed to notice Souji's silent reappearance with a bag of supplies and a change of clothing thrown over one shoulder. His eyes were flat and cold, unusual for one so warm and fiery as him, and a chilled shiver of fear raced down my spine as he handed my clothing to me. "Belima, do you think you can eat?" He handed the sobbing princess a small bag of nuts.

Unfolding the dress, a curl of disgust twisted my lips up as I saw yet another piece of peasants clothing in my hands, and a quick glance up at the supplies Souji had procured confirmed my expectations. "Nuts? Berries? Dried Meat and peddler's clothing. Have you forgetting just who I am? The princess of this court and the rightful ruler!" I stamped my feet against the flooring, the cheap wood rattling with the force of the blow.

"With all due respect, Princess. You're dead. The adviser issued a royal statement this morning that bandits broke into the castle and killed the royal family. He has proclaimed himself leader and will assume the position of high lord in a few days."

"It won't happen! I won't allow that traitor to rise!" I fumed, tossing the dress onto the length of the bed and resumed my stalk back and forth. There had to be something we could do, anything? But why couldn't I think of it?

"There's not much we can do about it now." Souji shrugged, turning back to my blank eyed sister and tried to persuade her to eat what he had brought.

# 5



With the morning came the dreaded knowledge that had been revealed. Seemingly overnight, black flags and banners had sprouted up like weeds, proclaiming the sorrow of the townsfolk over the fallen royal family.

"This is disgusting." I snarled at the next gaudy display of faux grief that looked like something fit for a theater. "They never supported us before, so why pretend now?"

"I agree with you, Lissa." Souji stepped aside to avoid brushing shoulders with one of the dark clad sobbing mourners. "It's disgraceful."

I let that one slide with just the slightest curl of my lip. With the declarations of the princesses dead, we left the inn at first light and Souji even managed to weasel a return of his coins for the nights we hadn't stayed from the innkeeper's fresh faced daughter. Although we were glamoured and dressed in our common clothes of a field hand, our images were too widely known throughout the court and someone could recognize us if they knew were and how to look through a glamor.

"Stick close to my sides, my ladies." Souji whispered as we approached the edge of the town, only to see that a check point manned by two sepia winged soldiers inspected every exiting person. Great, just great. "Do not interact with them and we should be fine."

That was easier said than done because they noticed us almost immediately "Well, well. What do we have here? Another bunch of ragamuffin farmers looking to scratch in the dirt for their next meals." The larger of the two swaggered up, the tips of his heavy wings brushing against the ground in a lax version of soldiers proper stance that stirred up a small cloud of dust that made my sister sneeze. The guard whipped around, focusing his glittering eyes directly on Belima. I subtly shifted my shoulder in front of hers, keeping my chin low but creating a barrier between her and him. She may be an idiot, but she was my sister and no one was going to hurt her.

I could hear the cruel smirk smearing his lips grow even wider before the soldier ever grabbed my chin in his hand and forcefully pushed my head up. My hands itched with the burn to slap him for his actions, but I curled them against the folds of my dress as his stinking breath bathed my face. "You're a homely little thing, ain't ya?" No wonder the boy's got two of 'em. Double the ass for what their faces lack."

Out of the corner of my eye, I saw Souji stiffen and hovering protectively over my sister, the faint outline of his twitching tails and ears almost becoming a shadow that outlined his figure before they faded into nothing. Instead, he reaching out his arm to curl around my shoulders and drew me away from the soldiers grasp. "Sir, please let us pass. Both me and my sisters are due to work in the fields."

"Really? Traveling farmhands, huh? Well, I'm afraid I can't let you go through so quick. We're searching for the assassins that killed the royal family, you see." The soldier narrowed his eyes, rushing forward with speed that belayed his girth to grab the hidden sword strapped to Souji's waist. "Like this. What's a raggedy farmer like you doing with a royal sword like this one? In fact, you three might just be part of the assassins themselves."

"My ladies, please run as fast as you can." Souji said as he backed us away from the guards and their approaching blades as each soldier drew a long silver sword. There was only a second of silence before orange flames rippled from his body, the full force of the fire Fae magic blazing white hot and able to burn anything in his path. He surged through the men in a blur of orange and white, the clash of steel against steel dangerously mixing with the screams of pain, the rank smell of burning feathers, and metallic blood until it churned my stomach to a dangerous level as I pulled my sister to safety. Still, a surge of panic rolled through my veins as one of the soldiers reinforcements dropped from the sky and landed in my path, but I couldn't even take a breath before Souji's sword had already entered his neck. A quick, sucking pop was the only effect preceding the falling bounce of head separating from its body before both items hit the ground in a clank of armor. "Please, come!" It was not a question, but an order that had my legs moving to Souji's voice as he followed behind us into the dark looming forest beyond.

# 6



~Belima~

Avalissa pushed onward through the forest, keeping hold of my hand the entire time as I tumbled along behind her like a doll. Scolies tumbled about underneath the fabric of my dress, his long squirming body almost ticklish and his muffled complaints were obvious now that we were away from the soldiers. I suppressed a shudder as we continued to run, the memory of the guards sneering face all too real in my thoughts. I don't know how my sister stood his touch, or not even making a single movement against him. I have seen her slap a man to the point of rendering him unconscious for so much as trying to kiss her hand at a noble event. But this... this was entirely different.

Desperate for a place to hide, we kept running until a large ledge created by an overhanging tree and a rocky cliff loomed just ahead. I tried to speak and point it out, but Avalissa had already saw it and pushed both herself and me into the narrow space and waited, nervously holding her dagger blade out and ready to slice at the first sign of danger.

The silence that followed was more unnerving than the approaching booms of wingbeats far in the distance, then the crunching of footsteps alerted her to the incoming presence of another person. Avalissa adjusted the grip on her dagger as I waited in silence born of pure fear until the steps neared and she strike out. Large hands easily caught her wrists, blocking the movement and casting her harmlessly aside less she hurt herself.

I let out a long sigh of relief as the familiar smile sent my heart fluttering with relief. "Princesses, it's just me." Souji approached from the shadows. His nice new clothes were caked in blood and ash, fresh smears of both decorating his golden tanned skin like the most garish of makeup, but he was otherwise unharmed except for an oozing slash on his left arm. Scolies welcomed him too, his peeping chirps almost bird like as he wiggled himself free of my clothing and scampered across the floor as fast as his tiny legs could carry him.

"You're hurt." I whispered softly, reaching out to run my fingers along the edge of his tattered sleeves and the newest gash around his wrist.

"It's only a small slash. Nothing you should worry yourself about, princess." He patted my arm and looked towards the dwelling. "Excellent choice. This should provide us with a bit of shelter till we get our bearings."

"But what about the soldiers? They'll be combing the forest for us." Avalissa scowled, suspiciously glancing around the surroundings like she expected the soldiers to jump out at any moment.

"Avalissa," She visibly flinched when a warning look flashed over his face. "Do not worry about the soldiers. They will not be troubling us."

A sneaking suspicion whispered softly to me that perhaps the soldiers were no longer of this world and based on the solemn expression on his face, that possibility was very real.

The brief overnight stay turned into days as we stayed hidden while the land plunged into a series of false mourning that just made me sick to my stomach as we watched it all from the safety of the forest. Even the funeral possession of glimmering orange lanterns that made its way from the heart of the town a cliff overlooking the rolling sea below.

My eyes refused to be torn from the scene as a lone figure in long black robes stepped to the fore and began to speak, each one of his muffled words blazing another ember of anger in my veins as the one responsible for this outrage. I would make sure that his feathers were plucked and his wings broken, the most severe punishment in the Wind Court for any trueborn Wind Fae. "My ladies, come. It is not worth upsetting yourselves over for a pack of lies." With a subtle splash that drew my attention away for a moment, Souji tugged on the line of his handmade fishing pole and a shining silver fish producing on the end of the line. Still, I shifted back up to glare at the scene above, silently wishing that the cliff would collapse and take the treacherous one standing there in the icy cold water below to be smashed and batted against the rocks until he was nothing more than a bloody stain to be washed away in the waves.

"A true princess would be leading her soldiers in a rebellion," My hands fisted at my sides, the wooden pole formed from a fallen tree branch crackling in my grip as my own empty line bobbed about uselessly in the water. "Not grubbing about in the dirt for a bloody fish!"

Souji looked up from where his fingers were expertly untangling the fish from the hook, his lazy smile in place as he watched the dark shadow of a fish linger under the water like it was considering a bite of his line. "True, but princesses should know when to bide their time and wait. Take a look at your sister, she's doing well under the circumstances." He directed his gaze to Belima who was carefully gathering small sticks for our fire nearby.

"What? She's scrabbling around for sticks and berries. That's hardly Princesses duties at all." A sudden tug on my line forced her my attention back to the pole where a fish twisted and fought. I gritted my teeth, digging my heels into the ground and pulling with all the strength I had. It was too much for the line, snapping clean in two and the fish darted away with its newfound freedom, seemingly encouraged my loud curses and the remains of my pole splashing into the water after it.

"That's okay. Even a tricky fish can escape the most experienced fisherman. It's nothing to be ashamed of." Souji's complement fell hollow as I added a few more curses for good measure before we tromped back to the campsite with only his fish in hand. Souji stoked the campfire, cleaned the fish of its innards, and roasted it atop the flames in a wooden split he fashioned himself. The smell of the fish roasting was fairly delicious to me, but the scent seemed to be having the opposite effect on my sister, turning her pale skin a vile shade of green and her lips pressed so tightly together that they almost disappeared from sight. She slumped against the nearest tree, her forehead pressed tightly against the cooler surface to try and soothe away the ache. At least that was until Souji held out his hand, a skewer of roasted fist held between his fingers. "Princess, are you okay?" Belima barely gave him time to spit out the words before she pushed away from the tree and ran to the safety of the nearest bushes, the sound of her retching much too loud in the quiet gloom.

Within a moment, Souji had descended on Belima once again, soothing pleas dripping from his lips as he held back my sister's hair with a gentle hand. I couldn't help my own lip curling at such a tender sight, glancing down at my own piece of roasted fish that now looked like nothing more than rotting coals. "Are you sick again? Souji, stop playing nursemaid for her and maybe she can actually grow a backbone."

"I can't help it." Belima, her voice broken by sucking gasps, replied before Souji could ever voice a reply. Her hand quickly swiped over her lips, smearing spittle and who knows what else as she pulled herself to her feet and leaned against his larger frame for support. "But I do have a backbone. I'm sorry that I'm not ready to go and risk my life on some foolish charge that would only have one result, death."

I scoffed, quickly biting off a chunk of the fist but it tasted like nothing more than sand in my mouth. "Like you've ever fought for anything in your life. The precious smaller princess only had to shed a single tear over a piece of smashed bug before you had anything you wanted placed in your hands."

Belima reeled back on her heels like I had flung daggers at her rather than the words themselves, small clear streams of pearly tears racing down her cheeks as her fists clung tight to the roughened fabric of Souji's shirt. "Avalissa, there is no shame in your sister being gentle," Souji's golden gaze burned nearly as hot as the anger surging through my veins. "There are some thing s that can only be accomplished by the gentle alone. Even the fiercest beast may one day subside to the gentlest strokes of a soft hand. You would do well to remember that." He gently stroked his hand along Belima's back to soothe the spasms still racking her body.

I couldn't take it anymore, not her constant crying or the way he was always watching over her. I stood up, lifting up what remained of my meal and walked to the farthest reaches of the firelight that flickered into shadows. My teeth snapped through the fish, the taste not even lingering on my tongue as I chewed and swallowed without much thought other than what seemed to be the most obvious truth of all. "You talk about facing facts, Souji," I whispered more to myself than anything, watching him tend to Belima with the upmost care. "Maybe you should admit that you're in love with Belima and that you always have been."

# 7



After Avalissa's bitter eruption, an uneasy silence fell over the camp like a deadly fog, neither of us speaking to one another. In fact, she barely spoke at all to Souji and certainly not to Scolies when he had dared to skitter across her path. The air itself was thick with tension, like a rope pulled taught and was threating to snap at any moment and give birth to irresistible consequences.

The increasing presence of Wind court soldiers only added a new level of stress to our already perilous situation. Patrolling both on foot and on wing, both attempts narrowly missed our hideout. Finally, Souji could not put off our departure any longer, not if we wanted to remain free. "Come along, my ladies. Don't look so sour. It's a lovely day for a walk." He teased gently, but neither I nor my sister would grant him the smile he wanted.

A grim frown had carved itself into Avalissa's sharp features, turning her nearly into a stone faced monster as she silently walked ahead with a brisk stride. My own eyes were reddened and swollen, evidence of the waterfalls of tears that just seemed to overflow every time I managed to find a few moments to myself. At least Scolies was happy, the small dragon chattering from his perch on my shoulder, sometimes reaching one of his tiny arms for a passing branch that left his upper body dangling with a comical swinging motion that usually never failed to bring a smile to my face but I still couldn't muster more than a slight upwards tilt of my lips.

The further we ventured, the more that I noticed how Avalissa was steadily studying the landscape as she walked, probably comparing it to the mental maps of the land that she had studied in the library of our home. Although Souji was my most loyal friend, excellent soldier, and was one of my father's top generals. His frequent bouts of direction impairment were in evidence as we passed by the same lightning struck willow tree for the third time within the last few hours. The faint strands of a curse bellowed low under his breath as he sighed, angrily running a hand through his short blonde strands until they looked like lightening had come down and fried his very hair itself. He paused, looking from left to right in an internal debate of which direction to try next.

Avalissa could stand it no longer, briskly marching forth into the lead and in what direction I assumed might lay the town of Quisree ahead, she barked a swift "This way!" before marching off. Souji tossed a half curious/half relieved glance over his shoulder before giving a shrug and following along as she walked down a dirt path packed firm by years of many feet, over the half rotten bridge turned green with moss and mold and suspended beside a roaring waterfall that sent blasts of water in every direction, and straight to the entrance of Quisree itself before she paused.

This certainly wasn't the city I had pictured.

According to all of the reports and rumors that I had heard, Quisree was supposed to have been a charming farming town filled with grinding mills for the grains grown and harvested by the farmers surrounding the town, but this town was in shambles. Everywhere I looked was half standing shacks and hollowed eyed people grown gaunt by life's hardships. Not only was I shocked but my sister was as well, her jaw hanging slack in a stunned silence that was beyond any amount of suffering that we had seen before. The one saving grace was a single farmhouse located on the western edge of town, a sturdy older woman sweeping the doorstep with a broom that barely contained any bristles left in its bindings. Souji made a silent hand motion for us to stay before he approached her with a friendly smile, their muted conversation taking only a few moments before he offered her a few coin pieces from his purse. The gold and silver barely had a chance to flash in the light before they were swept up in her gnarled hands, disappearing into the length of her skirt before she jerked a thumb high in the air, pointing towards a rundown old barn just beyond the cottage.

Avalissa let out a snort as Souji motioned us to come forward, but I really could care less.

# 8

~Belima~

"**B**lock it!"

My fingertips paused just under Scolies neck spikes as Avalissa swung the dagger upwards, just barely blocking the downswing of Souji's sword just moments before it reached her head, as if Souji would have actually allowed the wayward blow to land but the clang of steel versus steel was all too loud to my ears. He drew back, allowing my sister to recover for a moment while he observed her bowed stance. "Your reflexes are too slow for true combat. You would be defeated in an instant." He murmured idly.

Avalissa irritably swung her dagger aside, the air whistling as the blade cut through with a lethal hissing accuracy. "It's because I'm not used to such a difference in weight. I'm a perfectly good swordswoman when I have a sword."

"If you are a true swordswoman, than it shouldn't matter what type of blade you use." The old woman whose barn we had been sleeping in for the past few days cackled loudly and flung a blade into the center of the clearing. Tarnished and scratched, the glimmer of Fae steel was unmistakable even to my untrained eyes. Avalissa picked up the sword, cautiously looking it over and testing the weight with flick of her hands.

"That's an officer's sword." Souji remarked, gazing curiously at the older woman who steadily approached with a limping stride.

Hidden behind the strings of her apron, she produced another blade from behind her back, a shorter blade but still Fae steel regardless. "My husband used to be an officer in the mortal branch of the Wind Court

35

army before he died, and these swords were his pride and joy. He taught me how to use them correctly. But now let's see what you know, little girl."

I felt it, the spark that lit a fire through Avalissa's veins take flight from the simple taunt. The hilt of the blade crackled in her grip, the loose ends of her hair flying about her head as she charged forward with pure fire and fury flashing in her eyes. A formless screech flew from her lips as she swung and battered the older woman's blade with a relentless series of strikes, but no matter how swift or strong, none reached past the deflecting blade to attack her target. The old woman continued to deflect back Avalissa's attacks with a lazy twist of her wrist, the smirk on her wrinkled face only adding to the deep spiral of my sister's rage. Even though I knew she had no wings, I would have sworn she flew at the older woman the way she attacked so fiercely

Still the older woman deflected each blow easily, disarming my sister with another quick flick of the wrist so fast that I wasn't sure it had actually happened at all except for the blade that whistled as it flew through the air edge over hilt, landing with a clatter in the dust some distance away.

Avalissa bared her teeth in anger, her eyes slitted and glaring daggers at the blade held to her throat. "You let your anger dictate your movements. That's a very unwise strategy for someone of your young age. You are too young to be full of such bitterness and let it rule your actions. If you ever want to be successful in your efforts, you will have to let go of your anger." The old woman nodded her head towards the blade lying some distance away. "You're fighting style reveals many things. Your courage, your mental status, and any ailments you may be suffering. A successful swordsmaster knows how to read these signs and use them towards victory. Isn't' that right, fireboy?"

"Yes, ma'am!" Souji added respectfully, only giving the slightest blink of acknowledgement that the older woman had guessed his Fae magic.

"Keep that in mind, little girl." She sheathed the blade and turned to walk back to her house, pausing for a moment only to call over her shoulder. "You can keep the blade. Heaven's knows you're going to need it."

# 9



A deep dark haze of dusk had fallen when I noticed something very odd. I was practicing my swordsmanship skills with Souji while Belima and Scoiles had been gathering berries from a nearby bushes, her frequent scoldings leading to my guess that the small dragon was eating almost as many as he shook free. At least until my sister's repeated calls of "Sco-Sco, come here!" accompanied her rump hanging out of the thick thorny vines in hopes of seeing the shimmering scaled body dozed off with a stomach full of berries. I rolled my eyes, the dragon was such a glutton for fruit that it wasn't even funny anymore.

My arm raised up, the blade in my hand ready for a strike that would rip Souji's blade from his hands when I heard a hissing sound from a nearby tree. I looked straight up to see Scolies perched on a branch hanging just over my head, his long spine arched with the miniature defensive spikes standing completely at attention. The little dragon gazed off into the distance with suspicious eyes slitted in concentration and a pink forked tongue flickering in and out to test the air for new scents. "Scolies, what is it?" Belima's soft voice asked, trembling with a high note of concern. It was probably just a bear or something else wandering by.

I should have known that it would be worse.

I froze at the first snap of a twig, my eyes darting from side to side as I swirled on my heel. Souji going on instant alert as the heavy drumbeat of wings began to thud through the air. A squad of soldiers gradually approached, cursing every time their large wings became tangled in the thick branches and vines that snarled through the trees. "Scolies, come!"

Belima whispered and the hissing dragon obeyed her command for once, quickly sliding down to coil around her arm like an exotic bracelet.

"My ladies, to me! Quickly now!" Souji barked out a quick order in surprise, one lanky arm easily catching a panicked Belima and curled her tight against his chest, his golden eyes quickly scanning the area for the first threads of the soldiers' arrival.

"Where are they?" I hissed, the hilt of the blade crackling in my grip as I searched the forest with my own eyes for incoming threats. With the powerful surge of my recent lessons flooding my veins, the blade in my hand ached to spill some of the blood that had betrayed my family and my court. I would make sure that they begged for a forgiveness that I wouldn't give. The debt only to be repaid in blood.

Then I heard the screams, the horrible keens of true pain and agony that no living being could match except for one of the dying. Icy chills grabbed my spine, freezing my heart in its bone chilling grip until I was sure that I was dead as well, but I couldn't have been more wrong. Somehow my muscles had kept going, following a frantically running Souji and Belima to the flaming source of leaping orange flames clawing at a night darkened sky. The Wind Court soldiers madly laughed as they kicked at the old widow woman's prone body, her arms cruelly bound behind her back and her body wet from the pool of her own blood that leaked from the slice in her throat.

Belima gasped, burying her face in Souji's shoulder with a soft squeak, but I could only watch as they destroyed this woman's home. An innocent woman who had not even truly known who or what we were besides Fae. The ridge of my knuckles turned white with fury, the blade hilt creaking under the force of my grasp and my feet started to step forward, fully prepared to charge forward and return some of the pain that they had caused but Souji's hand landed hard on my shoulder. "Wait, princess. This is what they want. They want you to become so enraged that you reveal yourself." His golden eyes returned to the fire, his own bright flames flickering deep within the burnished gold with the power of his unspoken anger. "As much as it pains me to say this. There is nothing more we can do for her now."

"But-"

"But nothing. The queen tasked me with keeping you alive and that's what I intend to do!" I flinched at his sudden sharpness, but Souji sheathed his blade and reached out for my hand, tugging me along into the shadows behind him as we vanished into the shadows of death and despair.

# 10



The fires of my revenge only burned hotter as our trio left the town of Quisnee and the lands of the Wind Court altogether. The border of the Wind and Water courts was a swampy mass of lightly dusted trees green with lacy draping strands of moss, bogs of mushy greenish brown water littered heavy with the frothing skim of water plants. The little rises and falls of the land created a playground of islands sloping down into the marshes only to rise up again in the next island. It was on one of these islands that we had stopped to rest. Both I and my sister stared into the depths of the smokeless flame that Souji had summoned before leaving to find ourselves whatever kind of edible dinner he could find. Truthfully, I didn't care if he returned with anything to eat or not, my thoughts were much more concerned with how such a murder had occurred before our very eyes. They were going to pay, as much as I could make them, they would pay.

"Do you even care that they died?" I twisted my head, catching the stoic glance of Belima as she looked at me with bright tears of sadness and pain glimmering brightly in her gaze.

"Yes," I nodded slowly. "And once we have our court back, they will pay for the pain they have caused."

Belima looked at me oddly, the firelight throwing flickering shadows on her face and her eyes normally so vibrant with life, were cold and flat. "I never knew you were such a heartless bitch." She hissed quietly. "Who cares about the damn court? Wherever we go, innocent people die in our wake.

The low blow of the words inflamed my anger to the point that I wanted to burst like one of Souji's fireballs. "I'm surprised you know anything at all. You've always been so useless that it hadn't mattered."

"You take that back!" Belima lunged at the same time I did, our feet and hands kicking and clawing like wild beasts. A shower of dirt churned up by our heels extinguish the fire and what little of their camp that Souji had set up was destroyed between our blows. Stinging blood dripped from the gashes carved in my skin by her fingernails and it was Belima who struck the final felling blow to my head. A stinging slap that rattled my senses to the point that I had to lean against a nearby tree to rid myself of the dizziness.

I didn't have to stay here, not with the likes of her. A spoiled princess who knew nothing of how the world really worked. So I gathered up, my blade and headed into the swamp. The pounding beat of my anger fueled heart burned out everything that I could hear, including the sound of Belima's calling my name on the breeze.

# 11



~Avalissa~

I paid no heed at the water hungrily lapping at my legs, or the mud that sucked at my feet as it tried to hold me in place. I trudged on through the heart of the swamp until the first strands of light tentatively prickled at my eyes. Confused with the call of sleep muddling my thoughts into a soupy mess, I peered into the distance and noted that night was quickly falling and that shortly away in the distance was the Water Court city of Fivinella. The strands of light being the magical lanterns that they and they only produced. It was like a giant party with the soft flashing lights, the pulsing drumbeat of the music echoing off the buildings and the waterfront, and people flowed through the streets like the lapping water clawing at the city's base.

I had heard stories of how the water Court was much freer than the stoic Wind Court of my heart and birth but this was so much more than what I could ever imagine. Humans, Water Fae, and every kind of mix in between bumped and jostled my shoulders as I weaved myself through the bustling city.

A man who was in every other appearance a human except for his aqua tinged skin and slightly pointed ears curving out of his shaggy dark hair eagerly called out into the air. "Come one, come all! Try your hand and see if lady luck has a special favorite in you tonight." On a small table in front of him, his hands were a blur as he rotated a series of fast moving cards around and around. A few people had gathered at the edge, the clink of their coins against the wooden surface only a movement before they too vanished into the depths of his pocket.

I was so caught up in watching that I failed to see where I was going until my shoulder bumped into another in a thick bony collusion with a slight man passing by. "Excuse me," The words fell from my lips right before my hand brushed against the short thieving fingers reaching deep into my pockets for any belongs that I might have had. .

"Stop, you thief!" I shouted, but the man was already gone, off to pickpocket the next person without even a backwards glance. My head whipped around, trying to locate him when a soft chuckle come from the nearest shadowy corner of the street.

"Your new here, ain't ya?" The voice nasally drawled as a scantily dressed woman stepped into the light. "You better learn quick how to keep those wandering hands at bay or you'll be working twice as hard as the rest of us." She winked, wandering off to advance towards an unsuspecting man ambling along the street. It wasn't until a few moments later that I realized the true meaning of her words as I watched the woman flirt with the man till they walked to a nearby building.

A prostitute. The woman was a prostitute.

Instant panic started to thrum through my veins, my feet blindly rushing towards the first open doorway I could reach just to escape this place. A hotel, it turned out to be. One that took every ounce of funds I possessed just to rent a room from the stiffly smiling innkeeper. As soon as I had a key in hand, I rushed towards the empty suites but once again I was stopped by a cold clammy hand that groped my hand and pulled my body against something very male.

A water Fae lord, completely drunken and reeking of so much liquor that my stomach curled just from breathing the air tinged by his scent, rubbed his hands all over my body in a squeezing rush. I squeaked, my cheeks flaming in outrage as I planted my hands firmly against his clammy chest and pushed myself away. He mumbled some kind of protest, his drunken lips too tangled to properly form words, but I felt the snap as his fingers caught on the string around my neck and pulled the quartz from her neck. The crystal cracked against the floor with a loud crash, shards of deadened silver flying as far as I could see. The illusion around my body started to shimmer and disappear, and I reached down to grab the remains of the shattered stone and rushed away to my room.

It was only once I was sure that the door was locked and I was alone that the full impact of the situation attacked me as the illusion dissolved into worthless grains of illusion salt around me. I was alone with no source of magic, no possible way to fix the illusion and the crystal it was stored in, and if anyone saw my true face, then I would most likely be murdered in my step.

I shouldn't have done it, it wasn't a manner befitting a princess at all. But the very instant that fat pearls of tears beaded in my eyes, I shoved my hands against my face and just cried as hard as I could.

# 12



The sound of rustling pulled my sleeping thoughts into wakefulness as I blinked open my eyes, my vision blurry from being so swollen and red after I cried, and I tried to focus on the outline of Souji's blurry figure sitting some distance away. He was packing, looking almost ready to leave if I had any guess about that.

"Good morning, Princess." He said simply without even turning his head, the greeting greatly lacking his normal Souji vigor. I forced my vision to focus and noticed the weight of exhaustion stooped his broad shoulders and pulling the edges of his friendly smile so tight that it looked painful. His golden eyes had dimmed so much that the bright gold looked almost a deep bronze, but still burned with a fiery vigor. "I've got to go. Your breakfast is here by the fire. Don't leave the perimeter of camp." He straightened, slinging the fully packed sack over his shoulder, and ruffled his fingers through the top of my hair. "I'll be back soon."

I didn't have to ask about where he was going, I already knew he was combing the forest for my sister after she stormed off. I started to shift my legs under me, Scolies awakening with a series of muttered growls as I dislodged him from my lap and I shuffled over to the center of the clearing. A mush of berries awaited in a small wooden bowl that Souji had left. I wasn't really hungry, and Scolies ate the most of it. Once he was finished, I started over to the nearest pool of water to rinse out the sticky remains from the bowl. I didn't anticipate that the water would make my fingers so slick and that the bowl would so easily slide from my fingers and shatter against the rocks. A quick curse formed under my breath as

I tried to pick up the pieces, each shard just slicing a little deeper into the meat of my fingers with every movement. They were just a traveler's earthenware but the bowls were too valuable to just casually break now that we were on the run.

A puff and a snort made my hands pause, slowly turned around to see Scolies rubbing at his snout as a coil of sudden fear tightened around my spine. His eyes were partially crossed, tiny hands quickly rubbing, rubbing, rubbing until... He sneezed. A jet of brilliant orange flame belched straight out of his nostrils and into the smoldered remains of the flames which now blazed to life with twice the vigor as before. I cursed double under my breath, rushing to snatch the frustrated dragon back from the licking tongues of fame and abandoning the shattered bowl in the process.

Unaided, the burning flames spread quickly beyond the clearing that Souji had dug around the space and into the marshy grass, quickly blackening the greenery and singeing everything in its path.

I crushed out the flames with showers of dirt kicked up from my heels, but not before it had singed the rest of their supplies.

A crushing sense of defeated stole the strength from my legs, sinking down to my knees among the still smoldering grass as fat tears started to roll down my cheeks. I was so lost in my sobs that I hadn't even heard someone return until the thud of footsteps in the clearing was all too loud.

"Princess, I forgot – what happened?" Souji rushed to my side, his strong hands quickly feathering over my body in a safety check to ensure I was whole. "Are you okay?"

"I'm so sorry for being so useless!" The words choked free from my throat. It was true, I was stupid and useless. I should have stayed home and just let them kill me!

Strong arms pulled me against his warm chest with a gentle strength, his chin propping itself against my ear as Souji's voice whispered in the softest of tones. "Princess, you are far from useless. You are the kindest, gentlest heart that I have ever met and you have a unique strength that stems from that gentle heart. You just have to learn how to use them. Now, no more tears." Sliding one thumb beneath my eyes, he wiped away my tears and kissed my forehead.

"Are you okay, Souji?" The words seemed almost like a sniffle now, but I shouldn't have taken for granted just how tired he looked either.

Still he smiled though, that same Souji smile that the sun couldn't have made any brighter. "Of course I am. It's my job to protect the princesses." I glanced deep into his eyes for a moment, seeing the exhaustion and determination in his eyes, and I made myself promise that whatever lied ahead, I was going to at least help Souji survive just a little bit easier.

"You're a good friend, Souji." I had meant it as a complement, but I didn't miss the way his jaw tightened at my words, a somber glaze settling over his eyes as a quick flash of something truly sad flitted across his features before it vanished.

# 13



I walked with my head down and her shoulders stooped over to hide my face, the posture of a common beggar rather than the noble princess I knew myself to be. The broken glamor flickered like the flame of a worn down candle but it stayed in place for now. If I was going to get it fixed, then I needed more funds than what last night's stay in the hotel had left me with. My eyes darted between the buildings, scanning every business sign that might have labeled the slightest need of an available job.

I was just passing a shop whose windows broiled a sweet smelling greyish smoke when I heard something strange, two voices speaking between coughs and one I recognized as a dignitary in the Water Court that had visited the Wind Court once. My feet stopped on a dime, pressing myself into the shadow covered side of the building and closing my eyes just to focus on those voices the tiniest bit more.

"Do you really think that Galvar is going to have the troops ready for the invasion?" One voice huffed between deep sucking puffs.

"Of course, those Dusk fleabags aren't going to know what hit them. By this time in five days, they'll be nothing more than a dusty spot in those woods of theirs." The one I recognized let out a loud belch. Ew!

"Hey, You! Stop!" Someone suddenly barked and my eyes snapped open, quickly seeing the approaching bodies of two soldiers. Their skin was a sickly blue color and the fish like slitted gills in their meaty neck were slowly pulsing in time with their breathing. "Why are you sulking around with that cape over your head? Don't you know that the rules have changed since the assassination of those air Fae princesses?" The soldier reached forward and jerked my hood from my head. I started to pray that the wavering control of the glamor held true, but I could see the flicker of unease in the guards' eyes as they slid over my figure and he started to speak.

"There you are, Sis! I've been looking everywhere for you! Don't you know it isn't a good idea for you to go wandering off by yourself?" Belima's glamored face was all smiles as she bounced between myself and the soldiers, effectively cutting off whatever he had intended to say with a glossy smile. "Thank you so much for finding her!"

I couldn't help but be in awe of my sister's subtle skill, easily seeing how the men bent to her will with only a few pretty words. The soldiers quickly waved farewell as Belima linked her arm through mine and led me away.

Souji waited just a few building lengths away, gazing into the window of a potter's shop as he pretended to admire a colorfully glazed bowl displayed in the window. However his sharp eyes missed nothing, not even our subtle approach as Belima led me in a roundabout path to his side. I couldn't hardly believe they found me, much less that Belima was able to remove me from the soldiers grasp with merely a few pretty words and a smile. Within the space of a few moments, Souji had whisked us all right out of Fivinella and returned to camp.

As soon as we reached the campground, Souji held out his hand in a wordless gesture for me to give him the stone. I slid the stone from my neck and dropped it right in the center of his palm, his fingers quickly folding closed around the edges of the fractured quartz. Silver billows of pure steam rolled from between his fingers as the stone crackled loudly. He held it for a few heartbeats until he then opened his fingers once again, the shimmering crystal now whole once more.

During that time, I explained what I had heard from the two Water Fae. Souji nodded every now and then, and Belima was mostly silent she held Scolies, but it wasn't as if I was avoiding the topic of our spat. "So the Water Court is already in alliance with the Wind court they are going to wage war on the Dusk Court. It's madness." The thick locks of Souji's golden hair shifted slightly as he shook his head in sympathy of such madness brewing such a short distance away.

"Yes, But it's also something that would be valuable to the Dusk Court as well." I let the thought brew for a moment, and then I smiled. That was it! That was our bargaining chip to get the Dusk Court's assistance.

# 14



A chilling shiver curled thick and fierce around the base of my spine as we traveled onward through the water court's bog filled territory, prompting my arms to wrap tightly around my ribs as I looked to see my sister doing the same thing. A quick flash of silent surprise danced through her eyes, but then she shrugged. Even as twins, the amount of behaviors we shared was less frequent at best, which made this all the more rare. Avalissa had started to speak, but a low warning growl from Souji quickly silenced her before she began.

Just a few steps head, the Fire Fae had knelt down, a palm spread flat and pressed firmly into the ground. His unused hand rested on the handle of his blade, one thumb flicking at the tip as he readied himself to draw it if necessary. "Soldiers. Approaching on War Kelpies. Five fae miles from the east." His warm tone was so clipped sharp that I flinched, Scolies raising from his perch around my neck and hissed. The blade was drawn from its scabbard with a resounding zing, his glamor melting away into ashes as the first sparks of dripping orange flames bloomed along his arms like the outline of an exotic but deadly plant. "My ladies, if you would, run ahead and seek shelter. There is a waterfall that guards the entrance to a spacious cave behind within the next there fae-lengths ahead. Now, please go!" His many tails stretched and curled through the air, the pointed tips of two pointing in the direction he had indicated before the sudden thunder of hooves finished his last words.

Kelpies, the specially bred horse like water spirits that only the Water Court Fae were able to successfully tame. There was no way we could outrun them, not here and not now. Blinding panic started taking hold of my veins, seizing a paralyzing hold on my muscles until I just stood there shock still. Although Souji was a very accomplished soldier, there was no way he could hold all of them off, not on their home territory. The panic lost its grip as the first soldier charged into view, a rippling wall of pure flame springing up from the ground from the embers of Souji's magic, but he charged right through. His charge wasn't without its consequences as the soldier's pain filled screams shocked my body into motion, turning to run in the direction Souji had said with my sister following two steps behind.

Avalissa surged ahead, reaching out to grab my hand and push me down, pulling me just shy of the branches when my head was nearly snapped off by the leaping black hooves of a war Kelpie. The Kelpie thundered ahead, each step powerfully churning the watery muck but now without the rider on its back. The headless corpse of the soldier fell into the shallow water, the head falling a moment later as it had been separated by a swift flash of Avalissa's blade. I blinked, not quite realizing that the blood dripping from the dagger and staining her trembling hand red was truly blood, but this time she let me lead her away.

Just as predicated, the waterfall was just ahead and the room behind spacious enough that three rooms would have fit inside. The clattering sounds of battle had faded into a pleasantly cheerful birdsong that chirped and drifted through the trees. In fact, a strange sense of calm had settled over the land, one that was broken by the sudden sound of stumbling steps. Avalissa immediately leaped on alarm, her blade drawn and ready but it was only Souji staggering inside. Two small daggers protruded from his right shoulder, their color so dark of a grey that they looked odd against his warm skin and he blinked twice before collapsing at our feet.

# 15



"Souji!" Belima screamed, instantly rushing forward to pull him fully into the shelter of the hidden cove. In just that short of a moment, he was limp and lifeless and lifeless as a doll but his skin was flushed almost like he body was blazing hot. I sheathed my blade, kneeling down to help her and the first brush of my hands confirmed my suspicion that he was indeed blazing hot with a newly born fever. With both of our efforts, we were able to ease him inside and into a more comfortable position while Belima's fluttering hands checked his body for more wounds.

I was sure that he was in safe hands, and I moved to keep watch by the entrance. The waterfall's spray kept my visibility low, but I could still hear the distinctive clatter of armor as two bloodstained soldiers searched the surrounding area. Within a few moments, the hunched figures had appeared fully within range of the water, seemingly observing the blood trail that had dripped from Souji's wounds onto the rocks. That's when I noticed that they began to do something curious, they pulled off their heavy leather gloves, exposing blue tinged skin with filmy webbing between the fingers, and placed their hands directly in the water. I felt my eyes widened in shock, suddenly realizing that the rumor I had heard was true. By merely placing a part of their body in the water, the Water Fae could see through any liquid surface.

I don't think my sister was prepared for the sudden movement of my hand landing on her own as she readied to pull the blades from Souji's back, but I wasn't ready myself for the sudden descent of her teeth into my hand as her fingertips brushed the hilt of the weapon. My jaw locked tight, steeling myself against the pain as she muffled a scream in my flesh. The weapons were iron, they had to be to evoke such a reaction from her.

It was in this stoic pain that I counted each passing heartbeat until shimmering waterfall darkened with the Water Fae's presence now leaving. Finally, mercifully finally, the wait came to an end as the Fae walked away without any further engagement.

Belima let out a painful choked cry as she cradled her burned hand and wept the tears that had been stifled from the Fae. Iron. One of the most lethal substances known to Fae and illegal in most courts had been firmly embedded in our friend's back with the intent to kill.

There wasn't much time to waste. I pulled the hem of my dress up and sliced off a swatch of fabric, carefully wrapping it around my fingers, and started to pull the dagger out of his back. Even through the fabric, I could still feel the stinging bite of the metal against my flesh. Souji hissed and grounded as the first of the blades slowly slid free of his flesh, sounds that Belima instantly tried to soothe by stroking her fingers through his hair. She watched his face with worry filled eyes as I cursed under my breath as the second dagger slid free to clatter on the misty stones below. A second round of curses spilled from my lips as I prowled through our supplies for anything to use as a bandage.

Armed only with a small towel cut into strips, it required the use of the both of us to bandage the unconscious Fae, but his danger had not yet passed. The iron poisoning was still in his blood and he would die if we could not get him to a healer quickly.

# 16



Beyond the reach of the waterfall, the forest was not clear just as I had suspected. In fact, there were more soldiers than ever that had arrived, establishing a base in the center of a clearing. I crept closer on silent feet, eyeing a group of five war Kelpies had been tied to rest. The giant raven black beasts could have been mistaken for normal horses in their current rest if not for the gleaming silver bridles fastened to their heads. I was careful not to let my dress brush against a single tree branch or bush as I slipped beside two of the Kelpies. Twice as broad as the most prize-winning stallion and as foul tempered as the most stubborn donkey, the Kelpies were a prized breed that were captured exclusively by the Water court Fae to travel through the swampy marsh of the water court land at high speeds.

That was exactly what we needed.

With careful steps as not to step on the first twig, stepping towards where their bridles had been tied to a tree branch with only the slightest nicker from the slightly smaller one to my left as a mark of my presence. The fastening ropes quickly came apart under my nails, one particular strand sliding free into my hand from the one who had nickered a greeting, a mare by the looks of her if I was guessing correctly.

As luck would have it, the soldiers were too involved with their boasting and other activities to notice that one of their treasured Kelpies was departing at my hands, the same hands that also managed to snatch a pack of supplies from a nearby slumbering man as well.

The return back to the cave was blessedly uneventful as both the Kelpie and I managed to slip by each and every soldier we passed. I would not have believed it myself if I hadn't seen it with my own eyes. Once we returned to the cave, Belima was still fretting with worry for Souji as the latter's fever still hadn't broken. He twitched restlessly on the makeshift cot, a stream of unintelligible murmurs coming from his lips as his brow was furrowed tightly in pain. Around my sister's shoulders, Scolies hissed and wound himself higher from her shoulders to the top of her head like some sort of exotic hair ornament.

"We should have him ride the Kelpie, it's the only way because neither one of us is strong enough to carry him." I said as I quickly adjusted the saddle with a few movements. The Kelpie didn't seem to take too kindly to my hands fiddling with the underside of her abdomen, one dark hooved foot nearly missing my face as I darted back just in time.

"Souji, wake up!" Belima at least followed my orders, gently shaking the slumbering fae awake. Souji blinked slowly, his fever glazed eyes hard pressed to understand anything at all. "We need you to climb up on the Kelpie." She whispered, her fingers gently smoothing through the dampened strands of hair clinging to his face.

"Can't. Must protect you." With a sudden charge, he made a grab for his blade laying just beyond his reach but I pulled it away just as his fingers tried to latch on to the hilt.

"Don't be stupid! Get on the Kelpie!" I ordered him in a voice that rang with the familiarity of my father's authoritative voice. Souji complied without any further complaint, his shaking frame requiring both of our strengths to support as he slowly swung himself up onto the seat of the saddle. Once making sure that he was securely settled and wouldn't fall off if the Kelpie should suddenly need to run, we left the protective shelter of the cave just as the sun's light started to dip low.

It felt like it was only moments before the thunder of fast churning hooves started to chase us, our feet running as fast as we could slog while the Kelpie bucked and nickered so much that Belima was almost pushed down into the mud and trampled flat. The tepid water splashed against our legs, soaking our skirts to our skin and the thick mud sucked at our feet but still we ran on.

Soon, the swampy land grew firmer and rockier beneath our feet and the trees grew thicker, their sparse branches filling in with thick leafy growth that blotted out the moon above. With burning lungs and grasping fingers, we charged straight towards the darkest part of the forest only to have a newer arrival of the Water Fae surround us, their silver blades drawn and pointing at our throat's when a second set of hooves thundered across the land and golden eyed dark figures appeared in the night like wraths released from the depths of Hell itself. .

"Move and you will die!" The Water Fae captain hissed as he turned to face these new arrivals, an eerily strange howl chilling the frost of fear deep into my heart.

## 17

"Well, well. What do we have here? Looks like it's a bunch of lizards that's crawled out of the mud." The first of the dark clad soldiers snarled with the same curl to his lips as the grimacing beast on his breastplate. Their armor was pitted and dull, but nearly invisible in the faint light of the moon above as it filtered through the thick limbs of the trees. "So be wary of how you speak lizard because my patience is short. What are you doing in our territory?" The last words ended in a growl that had his companions eagerly jostling astride their own massive stallions.

I couldn't repress a fearful shiver as I viewed the threat of the newest arrival with the same trepidation that I saw for the Water Fae, my hand instinctively reaching up to steady a rousing Souji as he tried to rise from his slumped perch. However, Avalissa viewed the scene with eyes sparkling with interest as to how this new event would play out.

The Water Fae Capitan shuffled forward on his Kelpie to match his opponent eye-for-eye, his lip curling up with a snarl to match his flaring neck gills. "If you must know, we were in the process of capturing three rouges who had disturbed the peace of Fivinella. We are deeply sorry that we did cross the border in our pursuit but we will be leaving immediately as soon as we are finished here."

The dark armored soldier leaned aside to gaze around the Water Fae, his golden eyes shining brightly in the gloom as he met Avalissa's solemn stare and then my own as I reached for Souji, his glamor breaking apart thread by thread and slowly revealing his true fae features. Those golden eyes slid back to Avalissa's own and I could feel something spark between the two of them, like the moment before lightning strikes in a stormy sky.

Unwavering, she met the fae's glare with a challenge of her own. Her chin tilted up to show that she was a fae lady of noble breeding, even if only by half and she had the blood of leaders in her veins. I saw the quick flash of approval in the golden eyes before he turned towards the Water Fae with a dark snarl. "Just what did they steal from who because you've certainly never cared about keeping the peace before?"" The Water Fae blustered, the slitted gills flapping in his neck as he scrambled for words that wouldn't come.

Without another word, the dark clad Fae slid around the Water Fae leader and forced them backwards toward the border. "It seems to me that it's us who've caught the thieves and as such, we will be keeping them. I would recommend that you run for the border as fast as those Kelpies can gallop."

The dark clad soldier's horse advanced till the Water Fae retreated with a disgusted sign form their leader, the drumbeat of their hooves the only sound until it too faded into silence. Sheathing her blade at her hip, Avalissa squared her shoulders and marched over to the leader of the soldiers with the burning gold eyes. "We have traveled far and are in need of speaking to your high lord as quickly as possible!" Her voice rang out clear and confident among the trees.

I had not expected that she would be met with laughter.

"Well, ain't she a demanding little peasant?"

"Yeah! Who does she think she is? A Princess?"

"I want to know what they stole? I bet it was something real expense." Another jeered.

My hands kept hold of Souji's shoulders, forcing him to lie flat against the Kelpie's back as he gave a disgusted glance with fever glazed eyes so thick that I wasn't sure he was truly seeing at all. His skin was slick with fever sweat, his golden hair plastered to his face and neck, and his skin was so pale and grey from the iron in his blood but he still tried to rise and fight for us. How dare they insult us when we had come so far and when he was in so much pain? "How dare you call yourself Fae as you mock you own who have come seeking your aid and ignore your brother who is severely wounded?" I whirled on them with fury hot in my veins, Scolies rising from his protective hold around my waist to add a threatening hiss to my words.

"I see no Fae here, only a trio of pathetic humans." The golden eyed one jeered.

With a nod to my sister, I grabbed the crystals from both mine and Souji's necks in the same instant that Avalissa removed her own. All three crystals smashed against the ground with the force of being thrown from our hands, releasing a burst of heated air that shimmered with the form that we had been glamored in before vanishing into a burst of silver fog.

A deadly silence ruled through the air as each set of eyes scanned our features. "Your highnesses, we are sorry that we did not recognize you." The golden eyed one drawled slowly.

"Apologizes are not necessary. We only wish to speak with your high lord and for our injured to seek medical care." Avalissa briskly restated our demand.

This time there was no laughter as they led us onward into the very heart of the Dusk Court. The trees grew impossibly thicker until every shred of light was blocked from above, the land soft and mossy beneath our feet. Here and there, rugged stone buildings were nestled beneath the trees, human and Fae mingling alike as they traveled from building to building, small signs marking each establishment passed by too quickly for my exhausted eyes to read. When our escorting party finally stopped before the largest of the buildings, three departed with Souji to take him away for medical care despite my objections to accompany him. "The High Lord is inside." One soldier growled, leaving us to tend to ourselves as he too departed and we entered the darkened interior of the building.

# 18



We stepped inside, the entire building empty save for a single throne that had seen far too many years was sitting square in the middle of the room. Then the sound of footsteps echoed against the stones was all too loud as a dark armor glad soldier stepped to the fore of the building and took a seat on the battered throne. Belima shifted about from foot to foot, too nervous to stand still under the Fae Lord's imposing gaze, but I merely inclined my head to the side in a light gesture of respect though my eyes were narrowed. It was the golden eyed man from before, a man similar in age to Souji and ourselves. His dark slightly shaggy hair framed a rugged face too worn for someone of our age, and atop his skull sat two dark tufted canine ears, and if legend was to be believed, a long furry tail would curl from the base of his spine as well.

"Princess Avalissa, Princes Belima. Please do accept my apologies for your treatment thus far, but I'm sure you could only imagine our surprise when two dead princess showed themselves within our boarders, glamored no less." The throne creaked as he leaned back, his arms folding themselves over his considerable chest.

"As you can see, the rumor itself was reported false and was spread by the very one who killed our family and tried killing us as well." I snapped, in no mood for any further games of this sort. "That would be the very one we had trusted to advise and is the new high lord himself."

He shifted on his throne, leaning forward to rest his elbows on his knees. "You are saying that the previous adviser staged the attack so that he could become high lord, if you all are to be believed. Which leads to the question, why did you come to us? We have no ties with the Wind Court or with any other. We owe you nothing."

I quickly mulled over a mental list of her options, recalling the years of diplomacy I had witnessed when Belima spoke up. "Because we needed help and we were told too."

"What she means is that our mother instructed us to find you all and that you would help us regain our court." I rushed to clarify. He gazed at the two of us for a long moment and I could see the puzzle pieces easily shifting in his thoughts. Then I pulled out my own nuggets of information by explaining what all we had seen and what we had pieced together ourselves.

"If what you say is true, the whole land itself would be thrown into the bloodthirsty chaos of war, slaughtering thousands if not millions of innocent lives." He murmured after I had finally finished my tale.

"Yes," I stomped my foot against the floor for emphasis, my nerves quickly growing irritated with the high lord's indecisiveness. "It would be chaos if your court was not ready. You should thank us for the warning."

He laughed, actually laughed at me and my ire quickly grew even higher until I felt like I could burst into flame at any moment. "You are a demanding little thing aren't you? Tell you what, you may stay as our quests if you both will speak before my council?"

"Yes, yes. Of course." I declared in irritation, one wave of my hand ushering him on.

Belima slowly raised her hand and the high lord acknowledged her with a slight nod. "May I go see our friend Souji? He was our guardian and was poisoned by iron. He was taking away when we arrived her for treatment."

"Yes, of course. Exit this building and walk past three more. You will see the healer's sign on the fourth building and that's where he will be." Belima departed in a swirl of her skirt, barely giving a nod of thanks to the high lord before he stood up and offered me his arm. "Allow me to escort you to the council, my lady?"

I accepted with a nod and scowl, trying to find exactly what was annoying me so much about this Fae.

# 19



I rushed as fast as I could through the streets, counting the signs that I passed till I saw the fourth sign of green and white with a mortar and pestle on the side. I brushed through the door in a single motion, surprising a woman with long mossy green hair down to her waist and patterned skin crackled like tree bark and if legend held true, could transformed into armor harder than any diamond when needed. The Earth Court Fae woman smiled kindly as I came to a panting stop, inviting me in with a welcoming wave of her hand. "Please come in."

"Thank you, I was coming here to check on my friend Souji? He was a Fire Fae who was iron poisoned." I babbled, my fingers twisting the hem of her skirt tightly around and around until the fabric threatened to break.

"Of course, you had a right to be concerned as he was in quite serious condition. Please follow me." She turned, leaving a cloud of rose scented perfume in her wake. She led me to a room all to himself, Souji laying curled in a bed on his side with strong shivers racking his large frame. I gasped softly. He looked so weak. The healer quickly nodded in concern. "I know he looks terrible, but he is healing. From what I understand, if it hadn't been for you and your sister, he would have died."

"If it hadn't been for us, he never would have been injured at all." The whisper fell from my lips without any effort at all. The whole truth itself refusing to be contained..

The healer quickly left us alone and I took a seat beside his bed. His hand laid there open and I reached for it. His skin was cold, so much colder than the warmth I was used to that a single tear slipped down my cheek, quickly followed by a second, and then a third. A horrible image started to form in my thoughts of what my life would be like if I lost him too, and then the tears fell without restraint.

It was just the faintest brush, but something chilled and rough brushing beneath my eyes. I glanced up to see hazy golden eyes peering up at me as he tried to wipe my tears away, his hand trembling so badly that he could barely hold it up. "Princess, please don't cry. I can't stand to see you cry." Souji whispered, his voice so hoarse and raw that it sounded painful even to my ears.

"I was worried about you, so worried that you'd die and leave me alone." I snuffled, feeling almost as pathetic as I sure I looked.

But then he smiled, still being Souji even thought his grin was pulled tight with the pain burning in his veins. "You're never alone, princess. Lissa is always going to be there for you."

"But your my best friend and-" I reached up and gripped the remains of the twine around my neck where his crystal had once hung. I wish we hadn't had to break that crystal, the one that contained his dancing fire that glowed like his eyes when he promised that he would never let us be captured. It was his smile and his laugh, and something else that I was going to die right here if I didn't tell him now. "I love you, Souji and I won't let you die!"

I squealed as his grip momentarily slipped from my hand, the worst thoughts imaginable so easily conjuring up, but he had only fell into unconsciousness once more. I watched him, wondering if he had heard anything I said when I noticed that his smile had twisted the edges of his lips even higher, and then I knew my answer. He had heard after all.

# 20



~Avalissa~

I walked on the Fae Lord's arm until I reached a very long building. A small sign on the door marked it as the council meetinghouse and it was quick to see that once we were inside, every council was always made of the same scowling elders sitting around a table. Memories of the past quickly flashed in front of my eyes, easy recalling just how my court's own judgmental council had always dismissed my involvement. Fortunately for me, the high lord greeted each and every member by name, but for once I couldn't remember the names if I had tried.

One figure, a distinguished matronly lady with her iron grey hair pulled up into a bun, nearly disguising her lupine Fae ears, and the wrinkles around her lips creased deeply with her scowl. I felt my skin prickle as her thorn sharp gaze swept over my figure from the top of my head to the soles of my feet. "So you are one of the Wind Court princesses foretold to be dead. I assume your sister is here as well?"

"Yes, but she is rather occupied at the moment." I returned her stiff greeting with just as much enthusiasm. "We had injured among our party and his lordship was grateful enough to send him for treatment by your Court's medic."

"Ah, yes. The Fire Fae boy raised in the Wind Court. Bertram's boy, isn't that right Ephraim?" The woman turned to an even older man, his beard grizzled with silver and a polished wooden cane in his hand. "Yes, he was quite the fighter that one. Otherwise those spoiled brats would never had made it here otherwise. "His bones creaked as he settled back into the comfort of his chair, the nicked tips of his scarred ears flicking about.

"I beg your pardon," I spluttered, exhaustion sharping my tongue into a weapon even deadlier than normal. "Yes, Souji saved my life many times, but it was at my mother's request that we come here and inform you of the deception that has taken place."

The final member of the council spoke, a tall man with a thick mustache and a barrel chest straining the buttons of his grey shirt. "You mean that you brought trouble straight to our door!" He slammed one meaty fist against the table. "Your lordship, you must turn out these Fae as they will only bring more trouble to our doorstep."

The high lord stood and crossed his arms over his chest, idly gazing around the table with the piercing golden eyes of his. "No, that is not something I am prepared to do. It would be as if I committed the princesses to death myself. If the princess would be-"He wasn't able to finish because the tall man spoke.

"The court cannot support a war!"

"You won't have a choice" I snapped, quickly retelling the events that we had witnessed with none of the gore in the details spared for the faint of heart. I watched as their faces morphed to shock, even the High Lord's even though he had already heard the tale before, and then finally to a disgusted pale green mixed with white.

"We will need some time to consider this." The matronly lady spoke carefully, disappearing into a huddle with the remaining members of the council. The High lord himself give her a subtle nod of support, a flash of wink creasing up one eye and sending a quick flash of heat through her veins. What was it about this man that inflamed her so?

And why had he not shared his name with her?

# Don't miss out!

Visit the website below and you can sign up to receive emails whenever Clair Gardenwell publishes a new book. There's no charge and no obligation.

https://books2read.com/r/B-A-KGFK-IZQKB

BOOKS 2 READ

Connecting independent readers to independent writers.

# Also by Clair Gardenwell

**Alexandra Van Helsing**
Bite Me

**Sisters of the Fae**
FoxFire

**The Scarlet Huntress**
Dawn

**Standalone**
Tell Me No Lies

Watch for more at https://authorclairgardenwell.blogspot.com/.

# About the Author

A life long lover of reading, Clair is a classic introvert that loves animals, a cool glass of lemonade, and a a thick book on her lap. She is always on the hunt for an idea for her next novel, her inspiration frequently coming after a nap or a binge of her favorite shows.

You can follow her at www.authorclairgardenwell.blogspot.com for all the latest news.

Read more at https://authorclairgardenwell.blogspot.com/.

www.ingramcontent.com/pod-product-compliance
Lightning Source LLC
Chambersburg PA
CBHW051006060726
47593CB00017B/1100